THE ULTIMATE COLLECTION

BY KATRINA NANNESTAD
ILLUSTRATED BY MAKOTO KOJI

ABC
BOOKS

For brilliant boys and girls everywhere.
Yes, that's you! – KN

To my wonderful family and friends
for their never-ending support – MK

 The ABC 'Wave' device is a trademark of the
Australian Broadcasting Corporation and is used
under licence by HarperCollins*Publishers* Australia.

First published in Australia in 2020
by HarperCollins*Children'sBooks*
a division of HarperCollins*Publishers* Australia Pty Limited
ABN 36 009 913 517
harpercollins.com.au

The stories within *Lottie Perkins: The Ultimate Collection* were
first published in Australia in four separate volumes in 2018.

Text copyright © Katrina Nannestad 2018
Illustrations copyright © Makoto Koji 2018

HarperCollins*Publishers*
Level 13, 201 Elizabeth Street, Sydney NSW 2000, Australia
Unit D1, 63 Apollo Drive, Rosedale, Auckland 0632, New Zealand
A 53, Sector 57, Noida, UP, India
1 London Bridge Street, London SE1 9GF, United Kingdom
Bay Adelaide Centre, East Tower, 22 Adelaide Street West, 41st floor,
   Toronto, Ontario M5H 4E3, Canada
195 Broadway, New York NY 10007, USA

A catalogue record for this book is available
from the National Library of Australia

ISBN 978 0 7333 4098 7

Cover and internal design by Hazel Lam, HarperCollins Design Studio
Typeset in Bembo Infant by Kirby Jones
Printed and bound in Australia by McPherson's Printing Group
The papers used by HarperCollins in the manufacture of this book are a natural,
recyclable product made from wood grown in sustainable plantation forests.
The fibre source and manufacturing processes meet recognised international
environmental standards, and carry certification.

Lottie Perkins

MOVIE STAR

CHAPTER 1

My name is Charlotte Perkins.

My friends call me LOTTIE.

I'm an exceptional child.

I'm good at nibbling toast into interesting shapes.

I'm good at dressing my rabbits to look like famous people.

I'm good at writing my name backwards.

I'm good at fogging up windows.

'You are an exceptional child, Lottie Perkins,' I say to myself. 'And don't let anyone tell you otherwise.'

'Charlotte Perkins, you are a DAYDREAMER,' says Mrs Dawson.

Mrs Dawson is my Year 2 teacher. She invites my mother to come in for a chat.

A serious chat.

About my daydreaming.

I'm good at distracting Mum
from bad things my teacher
says. I fake a dizzy turn.

I knock three books, an apple and the goldfish bowl off Mrs Dawson's desk.

Mum freaks out. Which proves that I'm also good at acting.

'You are an exceptional actor, Lottie Perkins,' I say to myself. 'You should be a MOVIE STAR!'

CHAPTER 2

'I'm going to be a movie star!' I tell my pet goat, Feta.

'BAA!' says Feta. That's goat talk for, 'About time, Lottie. You have real talent.'

'I'm going to be a movie star!' I tell
Mum.

'Stop shouting, Charlotte Emily
Perkins!' she snaps.

Mum always calls me Charlotte
Emily Perkins when she's cross.

Like last night …

'Come here at once, Charlotte Emily Perkins!'

And last Sunday …

'What on EARTH have you done to your grandmother's wallpaper, Charlotte Emily Perkins?'

And last Christmas …

'Did *you* bring that stray donkey home, Charlotte Emily Perkins?'

'I'm going to be a movie star!'

I tell my class.

'Don't be a PEA BRAIN,' says
Harper Dark. 'You couldn't be
a movie star in a million years.'

So rude! And nasty!

But that's Harper Dark for you.

She's a bully and my arch-enemy.

I'm good at ignoring Harper
Dark. Most of the time.

'I'm going to be a movie star!' I tell
my best friend, Sam Bell.

'Really?' shouts Sam. 'Well,
pickle my pants! What a great idea!'

And *that's* why Sam is my best
friend. He's kind and funny and
smart and says crazy things like,
'Pickle my pants!'

And he believes in me.

CHAPTER 3

'LIGHTS! CAMERA! ACTION!'
yells Sam.

Sam films Feta eating my
homework. He films it all the way
through.

'Why didn't you stop her?' I ask.

Sam shrugs. 'The light on her

horns was so pretty. And I couldn't

find the stop button on the video

camera.'

Never mind. No homework

means more time to choose my

movie-star costume.

'LIGHTS! CAMERA! ACTION!'
yells Sam.

Sam films me as I walk across
the living room. I'm wearing
Mum's best dress. It's red with
sparkles around the hem. It's short
on Mum, but comes down to the
floor on me. My shoes, pearls,
gloves and fur wrap are from the
dress-up box.

'You look fabulous, Lottie!' cries
Sam. 'Like a real movie star.'

'Thanks,' I say.

I flash my best movie-star smile at the camera and keep walking.

I trip over the dress and fall flat on my face.

'LIGHTS! CAMERA! ACTION!' yells Sam.

Sam films me the next day at school. I'm eating an egg sandwich.

I bite into the bread as though I'm angry.

I chew like I'm deep in thought.

I wipe the crumbs off my face

like I'm scared.

'Butter my boots!' cries Sam.

'You are a SUPER-DUPER actor!'

CHAPTER 4

'You are a HOPELESS actor!' shouts Harper Dark.

Harper stands before me with her hands on her hips. Jane Chang and Eve Roberts stand behind her. They all smirk.

Harper Dark is good at getting other girls to be mean. But I don't know why she bothers. She's mean enough all on her own.

'You'll never be a movie star,' says Harper. 'Movie stars don't scream and holler when they play dodgeball. They don't skin their knees. They don't eat smelly egg sandwiches. And they don't have stupid-head names like POTTIE LERKINS.'

I glare at Harper Dark,

but inside I'm feeling small and
ugly. Bullies do that to you.

'Her name is Lottie Perkins,'
whispers Sam. 'And filming starts
tomorrow, so she really *will* be
a movie star.'

Sam blushes at his own bravery.

Harper narrows her eyes.

'What's the movie about?'
she asks.

I stare at Sam.

Sam stares at me.

'You have no idea, do you?'
asks Harper.

We have no idea. Absolutely no
idea. But we cannot tell Harper
Dark that.

'It's an ADVENTURE movie!'
I shout.

'With pirates and sea monsters!'
yells Sam.

'And there's a love story too,'
I say.

'With funny bits,' adds Sam.

'And sad bits,' I say. 'People like
crying at the movies.'

'And scary battles with sword fights and explosions and aliens!' shouts Sam.

I chew on my lip. I hope we haven't gone too far.

'It sounds stupid,' snorts Harper.

She stomps away. Jane and Eve follow.

'Rattle my ribs!' gasps Sam. 'I think it sounds GREAT!'

Me too!

CHAPTER 5

This is it! We're filming a real movie. And I'm the STAR!

Mum's garden shed has been turned into a café. My rabbits sit around a plate, eating grass. I've dressed them as Mary Poppins, Queen Elizabeth and

Captain Hook. This is the sort of café where famous people come to eat and fight and fall in love and set out on adventures with pirates.

I'm wearing Mum's red dress again, plus the fur wrap, pearls, gloves and high-heeled shoes.

Feta is wearing Dad's shirt, tie and underpants.

'Take care,' I tell Feta. 'That tie is silk. Very expensive. Mum bought it in Paris. She'll be mad if anything happens to it. Crazy mad.'

'LIGHTS! CAMERA! ACTION!'

yells Sam.

Feta and I gaze at each other
across the table.

I chew a piece of toast into
a heart shape.

I reach out and grab Feta's hoof in my hand.

'Harold,' I sigh. 'I think I'm in love.'

'BAA!' says Feta. That's goat talk for, 'I love you too, my darling.'

I flutter my eyelashes and that's when I see her!

Harper Dark.

Peering through the shed window.

Smirking.

'Juggle a duck!' shouts Sam.

'What's she doing here?'

I dash to the window and breathe heavily. It fogs up. I write backwards: GO AWAY!

'That's sorted!' I shout. 'Back to filming!'

But when I turn around, a terrible sight meets my eyes. The rabbits have gobbled all the grass and filled their plate

with poop. Even worse, Feta has

eaten her underpants and is now

nibbling on her tie.

'No, Feta!' I scream. 'STOP!'

Feta bolts from the shed.

CHAPTER 6

I chase Feta into the garden.

Harper Dark steps out from
behind a rose bush.

'Shut the gate!' I shout.

Harper smirks and holds
the gate WIDE OPEN with
her foot.

Feta bounces out onto the footpath, chewing the tie as she goes.

I dash after her, but trip on the hem of my dress. Mum's best red dress. I hear something tear. I fall and my knees sting.

I scramble to my feet. Now I'm *really* upset. I'm cross with Harper. I'm mad at Feta. And my hair and clothes are a mess.

'BAA!' Feta trots away down the middle of the street. 'Chomp! Chomp! Burp!'

I chase Feta around the corner
and run straight into a crowd of
people.

'Help! Help! Get out of my way!'
I'm screaming and rolling my eyes
and waving my arms in the air and
pushing and shoving like a maniac.

'CUT!' cries a deep, loud
voice.

The crowd freezes. Everything
falls silent.

Whoops!

I've run right into the middle of
a real live movie set.

'Marvellous!'

A man wearing a black beret waddles towards me.

'Your scream is truly marvellous!' he shouts. 'And your clothes and

hair are a mess. A MARVELLOUS mess!'

'Thanks,' I say. 'I'm Lottie Perkins. I'm an exceptional child.'

'Indeed,' the man agrees. 'I'm Bo Bloom. I'm a famous movie director.'

CHAPTER 7

Bo is making a movie about a
giant gorilla. Today he's filming
a scene where the gorilla chases
people through the city. He wants
me to be at the front of the crowd!

'ME?' I gasp. 'In your big
movie?'

Bo nods.

Harper Dark pops out from behind a camera man. She's been spying on me. AGAIN!

'What about me?' asks Harper in a sweet voice. She smiles and smooths her perfect hair.

Bo stares at Harper. He rubs his chin.

'Sorry,' says Bo. 'You look far too tidy to have been chased by a giant gorilla.

And your voice is too soft.

Too sweet. We need raw terror.

Loud screams. Hollering.'

Harper kicks Bo in the shins and storms off.

Just then, Sam squeezes through the crowd. I whisper something in

Bo's ear and he nods. He plonks
Sam in the director's chair and
hands him a loudspeaker.

'LIGHTS! CAMERA! ACTION!'
yells Sam.

I'm being chased by a giant gorilla.

'Help! Help! Get out of my way!' I'm screaming and rolling my eyes and waving my arms in the air and pushing and shoving like a maniac. I make my way to the front of the crowd and find myself staring right into the camera lens.

'CUT!' cries Bo.

'Perfect!' shouts Sam.

Feta trots over. A clump of gorilla fur is hanging from her mouth.

'BAA!' she says. That's goat talk for, 'Sorry about the tie, but all's well that ends well.'

CHAPTER 8

Sam and I are at the movies.

We've just watched Bo Bloom's

latest film, *Gorilla Fear*.

'Pickle my pants!' cries

Sam. 'That was brilliant!

Terrifying! Thrilling!

And your running and screaming and arm-waving were the best by far, Lottie.'

The credits roll and my name comes onto the screen.

'LOOK! LOOK!' I shout.

'I'm listed as an extra.'

'Extra?' asks Sam.

'Extra actor,' I explain.

Harper Dark is sitting three rows in front of us. She turns back and stares daggers.

'Extra jealous,' I whisper.

'Don't worry about her,' says Sam. 'You're the REAL extra.'

'You're right!' I shout. 'I'm extra special! Extra talented! Extra happy! Extra excited to be famous!'

Suddenly, I notice that everyone in the cinema is staring at me. I giggle, then flash them my best smile. My extra-bright movie-star smile.

THE END

Lottie Perkins

BALLERINA

CHAPTER 1

My name is Charlotte Perkins.

My friends call me LOTTIE.

I'm an exceptional child.

I'm good at tying ribbons into bows.

I'm good at making my shoes squeak on shiny floors.

I'm good at balancing on garden walls.

I'm good at handling snails.

'You are an exceptional child, Lottie Perkins,' I say to myself. 'And don't let anyone tell you otherwise.'

'Charlotte Perkins, you are a MENACE,' says Mr O'Hara.

Mr O'Hara is our next-door

neighbour. He invites my mother

to come in for a chat.

A serious chat.

About all the flowers I've picked

from his garden.

I'm good at sneaking away

from spots of bother. I creep along

Mr O'Hara's hallway, out the front

door, past his sleeping dog Brutus

and through the gate.

Mum doesn't even hear me go.

Nor does Brutus.

Which proves that I'm also good

at walking on my tippy-toes.

'You are exceptionally light

on your toes, Lottie Perkins,'

I say to myself. 'You should be

a BALLERINA!'

CHAPTER 2

'I'm going to be a ballerina!' I tell Mr O'Hara.

'Get down off my garden wall!' he snaps.

I tippy-toe along the wall until I fall.

I fall down into the flowerbed.

Right on top of Mr O'Hara's
tulips.

'GRRR!' says Brutus. That's dog
talk for, 'Good try, Lottie. Practice
makes perfect.'

'I'm going to be a ballerina!' I tell my class.

'Don't be a PEANUT BRAIN,' says Harper Dark. 'You look like a mud wrestler, not a ballerina.'

Harper Dark is a bully and a kill-joy.

I want to show her she's wrong.

I stand up on my tippy-toes and pirouette like a real ballerina. I spin around and around. Until I get dizzy and crash into Mrs Dawson's desk.

66

❀ ❀ ❀

'I'm going to be a ballerina!' I tell

my best friend, Sam Bell.

'Supersonic sausage dogs!'

shouts Sam. 'Great timing!'

Sam drags me across the street

and points to a poster outside the
town hall.

> ## BELLA BALLET COMPANY
> performs *Swan Lake*.
> ### ONE NIGHT ONLY.
> Local children welcome to audition.

'You should try out, Lottie!'
Sam smiles. 'You'll get in for sure.'

And *that's* why Sam is my best
friend. He's kind and funny and
helpful and says crazy things like,
'Supersonic sausage dogs!'

And he BELIEVES in me.

CHAPTER 3

I'm wearing a yellow tutu and
a sparkly tiara. They are from
my dress-up box.

I pirouette for my pet goat, Feta.
Three times. And I don't even trip.

'How do I look?' I ask.

'BAA!' says Feta. That's goat

talk for, 'Perfect! Except for the

sneakers.'

I flit on tippy-toes all the way to

my bedroom.

I stand before the mirror and hum the tune from *Swan Lake*.

I cup my hands in front of my tummy. I point my knees and toes outwards and bob slowly up and down.

I lift my hands and leap about the room like a gazelle.

I tuck my hands behind my back and balance on one foot. I hold the pose and smile at my imaginary audience. Even though I can feel something tugging at my tutu.

Because a true ballerina needs to
focus on her art.

'Well done, Lottie Perkins,' I say
to myself. 'You are an exceptional
ballerina.'

'BAA!' says Feta. That's goat talk for, 'Delicious! Light and fluffy, like a meringue!'

Feta has just eaten the skirt off the back of my tutu!

CHAPTER 4

The town hall is BUZZING.

Everyone wants to audition for

the ballet.

Except for Sam. He wants to

work backstage.

Harper Dark is here, wearing a

pink tutu and proper ballet shoes.

Pretty pink ribbons crisscross up to her knees. Her hair is pulled back into a perfect bun.

Harper stares at my scruffy tutu and sneakers. She rolls her eyes and nudges Eve Roberts in the side. Eve giggles.

My cheeks burn and my legs feel wobbly. Ballerinas need strong legs.

'Don't worry, Lottie,' whispers Sam. 'It's all about TALENT, not tutus.'

He's right!

I flash him a brave smile
and remind myself that I am an
exceptional child.

Madame Mimi claps her hands.

The piano begins to play.

Girls and boys tippy-toe across the stage, as light as butterflies. Everyone stops and stares.

My sneakers are squeaking!

The music changes. Children leap and fly and sashay across the stage. I leap too far and crash into Raj Singh. His nose bleeds. His big sister yells at me.

'PIROUETTE!' cries Madame Mimi.

I close my eyes and spin. Faster
and faster.

Until I get tangled in the
curtains at the edge of the stage.

Madame Mimi mops her brow.

'I think I've seen enough,'
she says.

CHAPTER 5

My legs jitter. My toes twitch.

Madame Mimi is reading out
the list. The list of children who
will perform in *Swan Lake*.

'First Little Swan – HARPER
DARK!'

Harper Dark squeals and fans her face. She runs up onto the stage. She bows and blows kisses to everyone. First Little Swan is the BEST role of all.

Soon, Harper is joined by nine other children, all Little Swans.

My heart sinks. My shoulders slump.

I've missed out.

I trudge across the hall.

I'm almost out the door when Sam grabs me by the hand.

'Wait, Lottie!' shouts Sam. 'YOU GOT IN!'

I, Lottie Perkins, have been given the role of First Tree. I don't know whether to be happy or horrified.

'First Tree?' I gasp.

'*Only* tree,' says Sam. 'But there's

a proper costume and you still get
to be onstage.'

Sam's right. I make a choice,
there and then.

I stand up tall and smile.

'I'm going to be the best dancing
tree ever!' I cry.

CHAPTER 6

Trees don't dance. They don't even MOVE.

I stand onstage, stuck inside a giant wooden tree. Only my face can be seen through a hole in the trunk.

Harper Dark dances past, gloating.

'You must be *so* embarrassed,'
she says.

Harper is wearing the most
beautiful costume I have ever seen.
It's a white tutu with a skirt made
entirely of feathers. Big, fluffy

white feathers. On her head is a
tiara made of pearls. Her ballet
shoes are white with silver ribbons.

SILVER ribbons!

I watch ten Little Swans flit and
leap and pirouette across the stage.

I could have danced like that.

I just needed a little more practice.

It's break time. I'm freed from

the tree.

I stretch my arms and legs.

I look around to make sure

no-one is watching, then I dance. I

flit and leap and pirouette, as though

I am First Little Swan in *Swan Lake*.

'You are a HOPELESS

ballerina!' snaps Harper Dark.

Harper has been spying on me from behind the curtains! Three Little Swans peep out beside her.

They are all giggling.

At me.

'You should stick to being a tree,' says Harper. 'A big, stupid, ugly TREE.'

CHAPTER 7

'I'm going to be the most
beautiful and talented tree ever,'
I say.

'Good for you, Lottie!' cries
Sam. 'I'll help in any way I can.'

'Thank you,' I say. 'I need
some snails.'

I hand him an empty jam jar.

I creep around Mr O'Hara's
garden, picking flowers. Lots and
lots of flowers.

As I go, I hum the music from
Swan Lake. I imagine I am First
Little Swan. I sashay across the
daffodils. I leap over the tulips.
I pirouette through the violets.

'GRRR!' says Brutus, baring
his fangs. That's dog talk for,

'You're a wonderful ballerina,
Lottie Perkins.'

'I know,' I say. 'But for now,
I am a tree and I just have to make
the best of things.'

I bath Feta and blow-dry her hair.

Feta hates baths. I feed her a
cake of soap and she forgives me.
She'd like to eat the rubber duck,
but I keep it for myself.

CHAPTER 8

Sam, Feta and I arrive at the

town hall early. We tie bunches

of flowers all over the tree.

Sam climbs a ladder and sits the

rubber duck in the highest branch.

I tie Feta to the trunk and plop live

snails on the leaves.

We stand back and admire our
work.

'PICKLE MY PANTS!' cries Sam.
'You'll be the best tree ever, Lottie.'

While we wait for the others
to arrive, Sam plays the piano.
It's just 'Chopsticks', but I don't
mind. A good ballerina can
dance to any tune.

I dance the part of First
Little Swan. I tippy-toe and flit.

I sashay and leap. I pirouette like a spinning top.

'What a goose!' shouts Harper Dark.

Sam stops playing.

I stop spinning.

All ten Little Swans are standing in front of the stage, smirking at me.

My cheeks burn. My eyes sting.

Harper stomps up the stairs.

'This is how *you* dance, POTTIE LERKINS,' she says.

Harper plods and limps across the stage.

She spins and wobbles, her arms and legs thrashing all over the place.

She goes cross-eyed and lets her tongue hang out to one side.

She grunts and heaves and leaps.

She slips on a runaway snail and tumbles off the stage.

CRACK!

Harper has broken her leg.

CHAPTER 9

'Tragedy!' cries Madame Mimi. 'We must cancel the ballet.'

'What if we find a NEW First Little Swan?' asks Sam.

Madame Mimi ponders the idea.

'It would need to be someone who knows all of the steps,' she says.

'Someone who has practised day and night.'

Madame Mimi scratches her head.

Feta eats a snail.

Three Little Swans weep.

'Butter my boots!' shouts Sam. 'I know JUST the person!'

CHAPTER 10

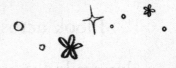

I stand in the wings, butterflies in
my tummy, joy in my heart.

I'm wearing a white tutu with
a skirt made entirely of feathers.
Big, fluffy white feathers. On my
head is a tiara made of pearls.

My ballet shoes are white with silver ribbons. I have tied them in perfect bows beneath my knees.

I look across at the tree. It no longer looks beautiful. The flowers are wilting. Feta has eaten the rubber duck. And the face that stares from the hole in the trunk is UGLY with rage.

Harper Dark is First Tree.

The orchestra begins to play.

Sam opens the red velvet curtains.

The spotlight beams.

This is it! Bella Ballet Company
presents *Swan Lake*.

I flit across the stage on my tippy-toes. Nine Little Swans follow. Our feathers flutter as we glide around the silver lake. Swan Lake.

The audience sighs in delight.

I pirouette to the front of the stage and wave my hand.

I am First Little Swan.

I am the HAPPIEST ballerina in the world.

THE END

Lottie Perkins

POP SINGER

CHAPTER 1

My name is Charlotte Perkins.

My friends call me LOTTIE.

I'm an exceptional child.

I'm good at building towers out
of library books.

I'm good at making up new
words to old songs.

I'm good at moonwalking.

I'm good at using glitter glue to brighten things up.

'You are an exceptional child, Lottie Perkins,' I say to myself. 'And don't let anyone tell you otherwise.'

♪ ♪ ♪

'Charlotte Perkins, you are a RATBAG!' shouts Mrs Monty.

Mrs Monty is the librarian. Librarians should *not* shout.

Mrs Monty invites my mother to come in for a chat.

A serious chat.

About the giant tower I made from books. The one that toppled over and hit Gemma Watson on the head.

I'm good at drowning out yucky words. I find a song on Mum's phone and sing along. Loudly. So loudly that Mum can't hear a word that Mrs Monty says.

Which proves that I'm also good at singing.

'You have an exceptional voice, Lottie Perkins,' I say to myself. 'You should be a POP SINGER!'

CHAPTER 2

'I'm going to be a pop singer!' I tell
my pet goat, Feta.

'BAA!' says Feta. That's goat
talk for, 'Fantastic! Can I be
back-up vocals?'

'I'm going to be a pop singer!' I tell
Gemma Watson.

Gemma smiles. And then her
eyes roll back into her head.

I think she has a sore brain.

The book tower *was* quite heavy.

♪ ♪ ♪

'I'm going to be a pop singer!' I tell
my class.

'Don't be a STUPID HEAD,' says
Harper Dark. 'You sing like a frog
with a mouthful of worms.'

Harper Dark is a bully. She tries
to steal my happiness.

Sometimes she succeeds.

♪ ♪ ♪

'I'm going to be a pop singer!' I tell
my best friend, Sam Bell.

126

'Groovy poodles!' shouts Sam.

'*I'll* be your drummer!'

We high-five.

We knuckle-bump.

We belly-slam.

We moonwalk.

We hug.

And *that's* why Sam's my best friend. He's kind and funny and cool and says crazy things like, 'Groovy poodles!'

And he BELIEVES in me.

CHAPTER 3

'Introducing Lottie and the Groovy Poodles!' shouts Sam.

Sam and Feta are the Groovy Poodles. I'm Lottie, of course.

'LET'S JAM,' says Sam. That's groovy talk for, 'Let's make some music.'

We're jamming in my garage.

I sing along to the radio. Sam plays
the drums he got for his birthday.

Feta is supposed to be back-up
vocals. She eats a ball of string
and half a bag of potting mix.

She head–butts a bucket. She jumps into the wheelbarrow and leaps onto the roof of Mum's car.

'BAA!' says Feta.

'It's no good,' I say. 'Back-up vocals should sound sweeter. Less goaty.'

'I've got it!' says Sam. 'Feta can play the tambourine!'

Lottie and the Groovy Poodles jam every afternoon. Sam rocks

on the drums. Feta jingles with
a tambourine around her neck.
I sing at the top of my lungs.

Brutus, the dog next door,
howls along. He howls and howls
the whole time I sing. He must
really like what he hears.

'Pickle my pants!' shouts Sam.

'I think we're ready!'

'Ready for what?' I ask.

'Ready to PERFORM,' says
Sam. 'I've signed us up for Our
Town Has Talent.'

CHAPTER 4

The talent quest is going to
be bigger than ever this year.
Tiffany Flip is giving a live
concert after the finals.

TIFFANY FLIP!

The famous pop star.

My favourite pop star in the
whole wide world.

♪ ♪ ♩

'I have the best idea ever!' I
shout. 'Let's perform "Strawberry
Dreams" by Tiffany Flip.'

'I love that song!' says Sam.

'Me too,' I say. 'And I know
almost all of the words.'

Sam gives a drum roll, then
bangs his sticks together.

'BEST idea ever!' shouts Sam.

138

'That's the DUMBEST idea ever!'
says Harper Dark. 'You will sound
like a kookaburra singing with
a beak full of lizards.'

'Kookaburras can't sing,' I say. 'They laugh.'

'Exactly!' cries Harper. '*You* can't sing either, POTTIE LERKINS.'

Harper Dark smirks. She makes Jane Chang and Eve Roberts smirk too. Harper Dark is the Queen of Mean.

My cheeks burn.

But I don't say another word. I'm saving my voice for the talent quest.

CHAPTER 5

This is it! Round One of Our Town Has Talent.

Sam, Feta and I sit on the grass with the audience while we wait our turn.

The outdoor stage is alive with talent.

Mr O'Hara and Brutus perform circus tricks. Mr O'Hara rides a tiny bike and juggles balls. Brutus leaps through hoops.

Kiara, Raj and Zara Singh perform part of *The Nutcracker* ballet.

Tommy Smith's entire family sing their favourite hymn.

And then it's Harper Dark's turn.

Harper is performing alone.

Harper doesn't like SHARING. She doesn't want to share the stage, the attention or first prize.

Harper is wearing a frilly white shirt and a pink skirt with flowers. Her hair is in two long braids.

Harper holds her hands in front of her chest and yodels. She yodels high and low, fast and slow, until the park is ringing with music. We all imagine ourselves skipping through the Swiss Alps with flowers in our hair.

It's splendid. TRULY splendid.

Harper bows.

The judges pass her a gold card.
The gold card that means she is
into the finals.

CHAPTER 6

'You look DRASTIC FANTASTIC, Lottie,' says Sam.

I've just changed into my costume. I'm wearing red shorts and a white T-shirt with a giant strawberry on the front.

The shorts and the strawberry are covered in red glitter. I spent hours gluing it on.

Feta has red ribbons dangling from her horns.

Sam is wearing a torn T-shirt and jeans and has a red cap on back to front.

We look like a real pop band.

'Ready?' I ask.

'Ready spaghetti,' says Sam.

We hug and run onto the stage.

'Strawberry dreams on my cupcake

pillow!'

We're ROCKING this song!

Sam is drumming like a star.

Feta springs about, her ribbons flapping, her tambourine jingling.

I'm singing and dancing in a strawberry-dream bubble. The sunbeams hit my glitter and strawberry sparkles fly out all around me. I forget the words, but make up new ones to fill in the gaps. I smile and sing the final verse at the top of my lungs.

We're almost finished when Feta spots a lady with roses on her hat.

'BAA!' says Feta. That's goat talk for, 'Yum! Roses are my favourite food!'

Feta bounces forward and leaps off the stage. She crowd-surfs her way to the hat and the audience loves it.

We finish our song to noisy cheers and wild clapping.

The judges pass us a gold card.

CHAPTER 7

The finals are in one hour.

Us versus Harper Dark.

I tie Feta to a tree. Sam and I
play on the big slide at the other
end of the park.

'This is the best day of my life,'
I say. 'We're going to win with

"Strawberry Dreams", then we're going to see Tiffany Flip perform the very same song!'

'Best day ever!' agrees Sam.

'DISASTER!' shouts Harper Dark.

Harper drags us to the stage and points. The skin on Sam's drum is torn.

'My drum!' cries Sam.

'I'm *so* sorry,' says Harper. 'I thought it was a chair and sat on it.'

Harper doesn't sound sorry
at all.

Feta is standing beside my
backpack, chewing a piece of red
fabric. She has glitter stuck to her
nose.

'My costume!' I cry. 'Feta's
eaten it!'

'I'm *so* sorry,' says Harper.
'I tripped on Feta's rope and it
came free.'

Harper smirks into her hand.
'BAA!' says Feta. 'BURP!'

Feta's eyes roll back into her head. Just like Gemma Watson's did when my book tower fell on top of her.

'Oh no!' I cry. 'The glitter glue has made her sick!'

Feta staggers sideways and falls off the stage.

SPLAT!

CHAPTER 8

My heart is broken. Feta's head is in my lap. I'm stroking her ears.

'BURP!' says Feta.

'She'll be fine after a good night's sleep,' says the vet. 'You got her here just in time.'

I begin to cry. I sob and sob.

'Truly,' says the vet.

I smile through my tears.

I'm glad that Feta is okay, but I'm still sad. I've missed the finals of Our Town Has Talent.

Harper Dark has WON.

CHAPTER 9

'Cheer up, Lottie!' says Sam.

'Tiffany Flip is about to perform.

We can still make it if we hurry.'

Sam drags me by the hand.

Across the park.

Through the crowd.

Around the back of the stage.

Until we come face to face

with Tiffany Flip.

TIFFANY FLIP!

♪ ♪ ♪

'Hiya!' says Tiffany, smiling.

'You must be Lottie Perkins.

I've heard all about you.'

Tiffany winks at Sam.

He blushes.

'Sam told me about the

competition and your poor little

goat,' says Tiffany.

I stare, mouth open. I can't say a word.

'Sam says you know almost all of the words to "Strawberry Dreams",' says Tiffany.

I nod. But, still, I can't say a word. I am dazzled.

'SUPER!' shouts Tiffany. 'You'd better see Costume and Make-up. We're on in five minutes.'

CHAPTER 10

I skip onto the stage, hand in hand
with Tiffany Flip.

Tiffany waves.

The crowd screams.

Sam beats on the drums and the
band joins in. A real live pop band.

With a keyboard and electric guitars.

Tiffany Flip and I burst into song: 'Strawberry dreams on my cupcake pillow!'

I feel FANTASTIC.

I'm wearing a white dress with giant strawberries around the hem, a strawberry-shaped hat and strawberry-red boots. A wide strawberry smile splits my face.

The crowd cheers.

Coloured lights flash.

Smoke swirls around our feet.

We skip and dance and sing.

I forget some of the lines, but I

don't care. I make up my own

words to match the tune.

I stare down into the audience.

I spot Mum, waving and dancing.

I spot a film crew. I'm going to
be on TV. Like a REAL pop star!

I spot Harper Dark. Scowling.

Green with envy. Even though

she has a big, shiny trophy in her hands.

I spot the lady with the roses on her hat and I think of Feta. Which gives me a great idea.

I toss my microphone to Tiffany Flip.

I blow a kiss to Sam.

I run forward as fast as I can and leap off the stage. I crowd-surf as I sing the final line of 'Strawberry Dreams' at the top of my lungs.

The audience LOVES it! Dogs howl. People laugh. The film crew zooms in.

Tiffany Flip cheers from the stage. 'Let's give it up for Lottie Perkins, pop singer!'

THE END

Lottie Perkins

FASHION DESIGNER

CHAPTER 1

My name is Charlotte Perkins.

My friends call me LOTTIE.

I'm an exceptional child.

I'm good at sewing on buttons.

I'm good at finding new answers
to the three times table.

I'm good at drawing pictures.

I'm good at eating chocolate biscuits in small, secret places.

'You are an exceptional child, Lottie Perkins,' I say to myself. 'And don't let anyone tell you otherwise.'

'Charlotte Perkins, you are a FIDDLE-POT!' says Nana Lou.

Nana Lou is my granny. She invites my mother to come in for a chat.

A serious chat.

About my fiddling. I fiddle
with her knitting and drop stitches.
I fiddle with the sugar and spill it
on the floor. I fiddle with her best
teacup and smash it.

Nana Lou's list goes on and on and on. It's boring.

I'm good at making my own fun when things are dull. I creep into Nana Lou's bedroom, where I find a pair of purple stockings. I cut off the legs and pull them over my arms. Handless gloves!

Which proves that I'm also good at making new clothes.

'You are exceptionally stylish, Lottie Perkins,' I say to myself. 'You should be a FASHION DESIGNER!'

CHAPTER 2

'I'm going to be a fashion designer!'
I tell Nana Lou.

'Good,' snaps Nana Lou.

'You can make me a new pair of

stockings.'

My first customer!

'I'm going to be a fashion designer!'
I tell my pet goat, Feta.

'BAA!' says Feta. That's goat talk
for, 'Great, Lottie. I could do with
a new coat for winter. A flashy one,
with pockets and three buttons.'

My second customer!

'I'm going to be a fashion designer!'
I tell my class.

'Don't be a BUTTER BRAIN,'
says Harper Dark. 'You'll never be
a fashion designer. You can't even
match your own socks.'

Harper Dark is a bully and
a know-it-all.

I look down at my socks. One is
pink with stripes. One is yellow
with white spots.

'I like my socks this way,' I lie.

Harper smirks. She sees right
through me.

'I'm going to be a fashion designer!'
I tell my best friend, Sam Bell.

'Brilliant millions!' shouts Sam.

'You can design my clothes for the SCHOOL DISCO next week!'

My third customer!

And *that's* why Sam is my best friend. He's kind and funny and daring and says crazy things like, 'Brilliant millions!'

And he believes in me.

CHAPTER 3

'Charlotte Perkins, are you LISTENING?' asks Mrs Dawson.

'Yes,' I lie.

Our class is learning the three times table. But I'm *not* listening. I'm designing a dress. A fabulous dress for Mrs Dawson. I'm drawing

it in my maths book. It's orange

with puffy sleeves and a wide skirt.

The skirt has giant yellow dots.

'What's three times two?'

asks Mrs Dawson.

'Sixty-four,' I say.

'Pea brain,' says Harper Dark.

'Charlotte Emily Perkins,
have you seen my red jumper?'
asks Mum.

Mum always calls me
Charlotte Emily Perkins when
she's cross.

'No,' I lie.

I've drawn a design for
Nana Lou's new stockings and
now I'm making them. I cut the
sleeves off Mum's red jumper.

I sew my pink socks to the sleeves.

I sew the sleeves onto Dad's green shorts.

I hold up Nana Lou's fancy new stockings.

'SNAZZY!' I say.

I chop up my best rainbow tights. I sew the legs onto Mum's red jumper.

I hold up Mum's fancy new jumper.

'JAZZY!' I say.

CHAPTER 4

I LOVE school discos!

A giant mirror ball sparkles above us.

The music rocks. It's Tiffany Flip singing 'Best Friends Forever'.

Sam and I dance together.

This is our song.

Sam looks so cool in the clothes
I designed. His shirt has six extra
sleeves sewn to the body. When he
spins around, the sleeves fly out
like a HELICOPTER.

I made my dress from a
pillowcase, but no-one would know.

It's covered in fresh flowers from Mr O'Hara's garden next door.
It looks gorgeous. I call the design *Garden Party by Lottie*.

Sam and I bop about and sing along to the music.

We moonwalk.

We do the Robot and the Sprinkler.

A circle of children forms around us.

We spin and giggle and have the best time ever.

Until Harper Dark ruins it all.

The music stops. Harper Dark
walks into the circle. She smirks.

'POTTIE LERKINS,' she says.
'What a fashion frog. Your dress
looks like a pillowcase.'

I blush.

'And where *did* you get that
shirt?' Harper asks Sam.

Sam blushes. 'Lottie made it,'
he says.

'Made it for an octopus!' shouts
Harper.

Everyone in the circle laughs.
Tommy Smith tugs one of Sam's
sleeves and it rips off.

I burst into TEARS and run from
the hall.

CHAPTER 5

I'm curled up in my wardrobe,
eating chocolate biscuits.

'I've given up fashion design,'
I say. 'Everyone laughed at me.'

'I didn't laugh,' says Sam.

I open the wardrobe door and
pass him a biscuit.

I sniff and wipe my eyes. I scratch Feta behind the ear while she eats three buttons and a reel of cotton. *I* won't be needing them any more.

Sam passes me a card.

'It's an invitation,' he says. 'To my birthday party. I was hoping you'd wear something exciting.'

I scrunch my nose.

'One of your own special designs,' says Sam.

'Really?' I ask.

'TRULY!' shouts Sam. 'What's a
party without fabulous clothes?'

I flash Sam my widest, brightest
smile.

I grab my scrapbook and start
designing my party outfit.

'BAA!' says Feta. That's goat talk for, 'Don't forget my new coat. A flashy one, with pockets and three buttons.'

'Silly!' I say. 'You just ate the buttons.'

CHAPTER 6

'Happy birthday, Sam!' I shout.

'BAA!' says Feta.

We strut down the path into

Sam's backyard. We look amazing.

We are both wearing *Winter*

Wonderland by Lottie.

Feta has on a powder-blue coat with pockets and a furry collar. Her hoofs are covered in woolly white socks with powder-blue bows.

Feta's coat looked so good that I made a second one for myself.

I wear it with white tights,
sheepskin boots and a woolly
white hat with a powder-blue
bow at the side.

'WOW, Lottie!' shouts Sam.
'You look brilliant!'

'Thanks!' I say. 'I made the
coats from Mum's best blanket.
I cut the furry collars from Dad's
car-seat covers. And my hat is
made from a jumper that Nana
Lou was knitting.'

I pass Sam his birthday present.

'It's a scarf made from socks and gloves,' I explain. Just in case he can't tell what it is.

Sam wraps the scarf around his neck.

'Butter a duck!' he shouts. 'Best scarf ever!'

Sam's mum, dad and three sisters stare at Sam's scarf. They are GREEN with envy!

Sam's birthday party is FUN-tastic. We play Musical Chairs and Pass the Parcel. We belt the piñata until it explodes with lollies. We do flips on the trampoline and cartwheels on the grass. We eat ice-cream cake and fairy bread.

Just when I think it can't get any better, Sam's Aunty Betty and Uncle Fred arrive.

And that's when the BEST thing of all happens.

216

CHAPTER 7

'Jiggle a pig!' cries Aunty Betty.

'Just look at that girl and her goat!'

Uncle Fred looks up from
his sausage sandwich. He stares
from me to Feta, then back to
me. His face breaks into a wide
smile.

'Hurdle a turkey!' cries Uncle Fred.

'Best pet-and-owner outfit EVER!'

Aunty Betty pats the seat beside her.

'Come here,' she says. 'Let's have
a little chat.'

'BAA!' says Feta. She springs up onto the seat.

I pull up a chair and sit in front of Aunty Betty.

We have a chat. A really big chat.

Aunty Betty and Uncle Fred own a shop called Pets and Stuff R Us. They have plenty of pets, but they want more stuff.

Aunty Betty rubs the furry collar on Feta's coat.

'Where did you get these SUPER outfits?' she asks.

'I designed them,' I say. 'And then I made them.'

'Brilliant!' cries Aunty Betty. 'Did you hear that, Fred?'

'Indeed!' cries Uncle Fred. 'Would you like a job in fashion design, young lady?'

'You can call me Lottie,' I say. 'And yes, thank you. I'd *love* a job in fashion design.'

CHAPTER 8

I'm waiting in Pets and Stuff R Us.
Aunty Betty and Sam are
flipping through the scrapbook
with my new fashion designs.
There are ten matching outfits
for pets and their owners. I call

them *Springing into Spring with Lottie.*

'I love the frilly yellow bikini,' says Aunty Betty. 'I'll need a matching set for me and my cat Fluffy! We're going to the beach this year.'

'I like the lime-green shorts,' says Sam. 'I'm going to get two pairs. One for me. One for my parrot, Lenny.'

'WELL DONE, Lottie,' says Aunty Betty. 'We'll have these made up in no time at all. Your winter fashions sold like hot cakes. These spring fashions will sell like hot cakes with jam and cream!'

'Or like dog biscuits with gravy!' says Sam.

CHAPTER 9

Sam, Feta and I are CELEBRATING
my success.

We sit outside a café, sipping
strawberry milkshakes.

The sun is shining. My best
friend is by my side. I'm wearing
a pretty pink smock and hat.

They match Feta's pink smock and hat. I feel fabulous.

Until Harper Dark walks by.

Harper stops.

She stares at me.

She stares at Feta.

She bursts out laughing.

'Pottie Lerkins!' she shouts.

'You are dressed like a goat.'

I blush.

The fabulous feelings FIZZLE.

Suddenly, I feel stupid and ugly.

A pink sports car pulls up near the café. The driver waves and sings, 'HIYA!'

It's Tiffany Flip, the famous pop star! I sang with her on stage once.

'Hiya, Lottie Perkins,' says Tiffany. 'Good to see you.'

Tiffany points to her poodle, then to herself. They are wearing matching coats from *Winter Wonderland by Lottie*.

'*Love* your fashions, girlfriend!'

shouts Tiffany. 'Keep up the great

design!'

She waves and zooms off.

Harper Dark stares, her mouth open. I'd say she's green with envy, except that her cheeks are glowing red.

Sam smiles. He lifts his milkshake and makes a toast.

'Cheers!' he shouts. 'Here's to Lottie Perkins, best friend and best fashion designer in the WHOLE WIDE WORLD!'

THE END